This Little Tiger book
belongs to:

....

....

000001045289

For Neil, who is *never* grumpy . . .
~ S J

For Ronald and Peggy — I've never known
them to have a grumpy day, ever!
~ A E

LITTLE TIGER PRESS
1 The Coda Centre,
189 Munster Road, London SW6 6AW
www.littletiger.co.uk
First published in Great Britain 2016
Text by Stella J Jones
Text copyright © Little Tiger Press 2016
Illustrations copyright © Alison Edgson 2016

Alison Edgson has asserted her right to be identified as the illustrator
of this work under the Copyright, Designs and Patents Act, 1988

The
VERY
Grumpy
Day

Stella J Jones

Alison Edgson

LITTLE TIGER PRESS
London

"What a perfect day!" smiled Mouse, looking out at the sunshine.

And goodness, wasn't he right! The birds trilled sweetly and the bees buzzed merrily.

"I'll take one of these cupcakes round to Bear," Mouse thought. "He loves a sweet treat."

Mouse tappity-rap-rapped on Bear's front door. But he didn't know that Bear had just left . . .

BEAR

. . . in a VERY bad mood.

"Oh harrumph!" grumped Bear.
"Bother these boots! They are just
TOO BIG!"

Bear stomped along so heavily that the ground shivered and shook beneath his feet.

STOMP!

STOMP! STOMP!

"Oi!" cried Mole angrily, popping up from his mole hole. "Your stomping has collapsed my tunnel. I shall have to start all over again!"

He flung down his shovel and had just disappeared into his hole when . . .

... **"Aaaaaaaaarrrrrrghhhhhhhhh!"**
Hedgehog tripped over the shovel
with a bump.
"Who left THAT there?" he cried.

He roly-polied across
the clearing . . .

. . . straight into Fox's bottom.

"**OOOOOOOOOWWWWWW!**" Fox yelped.

"Watch where you're poking your prickles, Hedgehog!" he jumped in shock and his bag flew high into the air.

The shopping tumbled out . . .

. . . and plopped all over the squirrel family!

SQUASH went the bag of flour!

SPLOSH went the milk!

And **SPLAT** went the eggs all over the baby squirrels!

"Be quiet down there!"
squawked Daddy Owl.
"You'll wake my chicks!"

Now everyone in the clearing
was in a **BIG BAD** mood.

QUARREL!

Up above, the sky turned grey and grizzly. A roll of thunder shook the wood and the rain began to fall.

What a dreadful day!

Stop pushing me!

Quick!

"Oh bother!" grumped Bear.
"There's a hole in my brolly
and my ears are getting wet."
Bear's bad mood lasted all the
way home. Then suddenly, he
spotted something.

"It's a present! For me!"
Bear picked it up and read
the note. "Oh, how kind!"
he sniffed.

And for the very first time
that day, Bear smiled.

As Bear munched happily on his cake, the sky turned blue once more and the snowdrops bobbed in the breeze.

"Mole would love those flowers," thought Bear. "I'll take them round to apologise for stomping on his tunnel."

"I'm sorry, Mole," said Bear,
giving the present to his friend.
"That's OK," said Mole.
And for the first time that
day, Mole smiled too.

"I should say sorry to Hedgehog for
leaving my shovel in his way,"
said Mole. He trotted over to
his friend's house and gave
him a huge hug.

The smiles and happiness spread like rays of spring sunshine all through the afternoon.

When Mouse looked out of his window, the whole wood was ringing with birdsong and laughter.

"Such a perfect day," he beamed, racing out to join his friends.

And it was!

More brilliant books to brighten your day!

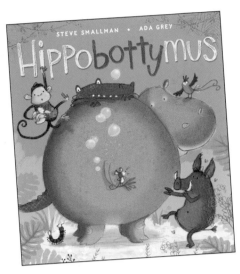

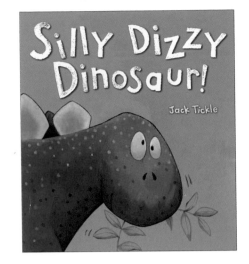

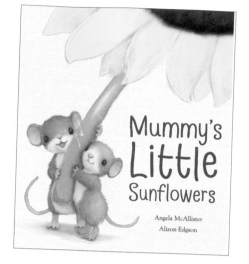

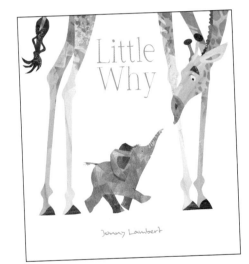

For information regarding any of the above titles
or for our catalogue, please contact us:
Little Tiger Press, 1 The Coda Centre,
189 Munster Road, London SW6 6AW
Tel: 020 7385 6333
E-mail: contact@littletiger.co.uk
www.littletiger.co.uk